The Annual Spring Costume Contest has been revived and Soup and Rob have high hopes for winning it. According to Soup, how you enter is more important than what you wear. But like most of their good ideas, Soup and Rob's plan for a grand entrance leads to more trouble than triumph.

But trouble is nothing new to Soup and Rob. Janice Riker, the meanest girl in town, is still out to get them. And now they have someone new to reckon with—Beverly Bean—who teaches them that names can be deceiving. Then Norma Jean Bissell breaks Rob's heart and Miss Boland almost breaks a leg.

Zinging with action and humor and filled with funny characters, these new escapades of Soup and Rob will delight SOUP fans everywhere.

SOUP ON WHEELS

SOUP
ON
WHEELS

by ROBERT NEWTON PECK

Illustrated by Charles Robinson

Alfred A. Knopf New York

THIS IS A BORZOI BOOK PUBLISHED BY ALFRED A. KNOPF, INC.
Text Copyright © 1981 by Robert Newton Peck
Illustrations Copyright © 1981 by Charles Robinson
All rights reserved under International and
Pan-American Copyright Conventions. Published in the
United States by Alfred A. Knopf, Inc., New York,
and simultaneously in Canada by Random House of Canada
Limited, Toronto. Distributed by Random House, Inc., New York.
Manufactured in the United States of America

10 9 8 7 6 5 4 3 2 1

Library of Congress Cataloging in Publication Data
Peck, Robert Newton. Soup on wheels.
Summary: Rob and Soup vie for the prize in
their town's "Vermont Mardy Grah."
[1. Vermont—Fiction. 2. School stories.
3. Humorous stories] I. Robinson, Charles, 1931–
II. Title. PZ7.P339Sr 1981 [Fic] 80–17661
ISBN 0–394–84581–1
ISBN 0–394–94581–6 (lib. bdg.)

To Chappy

SOUP ON WHEELS

ONE

"Florida," said Miss Kelly.

Soup and I were seated side by side on our bench behind our desk, both of our noses in one geography book.

"As you can see by the map," Miss Kelly continued,

"the state of Florida is almost all what?"

Janice Riker raised her hand. "It's almost all Pennsylvania."

Soup snickered, until Miss Kelly tapped the toe of her shoe, looking our way. She was going to separate us again if Soup or I whispered even one more time.

"Janice," said Miss Kelly, "meant to say *peninsula*—and that's what Florida is. A thumb of land that juts out into water. Isn't that what you had in mind, Janice?"

"Yes'm," said Janice, "because I got me an uncle who lives in Peninsula. Out in Pittsburgh."

Soup poked me in the ribs and I busted out a chuckle.

Ruler in hand, Miss Kelly took about three giant steps to where Soup and I sat. She didn't look very pleased; I suspected I was going to get it, and hard.

"Luther," said Miss Kelly to Soup, "it is not polite to poke a seatmate in order to create an outburst."

Soup looked down at our book. And that was when the tip of Miss Kelly's ruler slowly tilted up his chin so that he'd face our teacher straight in the eye.

"Yes'm," said Soup. "I'm sorry."

"And I promise you, Luther, that a certain southerly part of your anatomy shall become far sorrier if I detect one more meeting of your finger and Robert's ribs."

Shucks, I thought. Soup's not going to get the ruler.

But then neither was I, so I smiled some. Too late. Even though Miss Kelly didn't catch me, Janice did. Her big fist doubled up, and I saw her lips make me a promise for after school.

Silently, she said three words.

"I'll get you."

Unless I took off like a jackrabbit, right after the final bell, Janice Riker was fixing to pound me into a peninsula. Or maybe kick me all the way to Pittsburgh.

I didn't like Janice.

Nobody did. She was the most ornery kid in our school. Ugly mean, with at least forty-three knuckles on each fist. And her fists were near the size of bowling balls. But I'll say this for old Janice. She sure tried to answer every question that Miss Kelly asked, even though all her answers missed the target by ten yards.

"East of Florida," said Miss Kelly, "we find the Atlantic Ocean. To the west of the state another body of water, known as a gulf."

That was when Janice raised her hand again, to say, "My uncle in Pittsburgh plays gulf."

"That's golf," said Miss Kelly.

Soup poked me again, but I held on to my giggle with both hands, thus avoiding my meeting up with either a ruler or Janice. Then I noticed that Miss Kelly was smiling, which was always a safe signal that the rest of us could let out a laugh.

She was writing GOLF and GULF on the blackboard.

"Golf," said Miss Kelly, perhaps more to Janice Riker than the rest of us, "is a game. But a *gulf* is a—"

"Gas station," said Janice.

Outside, a horn honked. A familiar horn. I knew right away whose honk it was. Sure enough, less than half a minute went by before our door opened and in she burst.

It was Miss Boland, our country nurse.

Miss Boland came in only one size. Extra large. She was dressed in white as she usually was, and looked less like a nurse and more like an iceberg. She stopped in at least once a week to inspect our hair for wildlife, examine our skin to spot a rash, or depress our tongues. For that, she wasted a whole bundle of little flat sticks. Miss Boland must have eaten a pile of popsicles.

"Good news!" wheezed Miss Boland, hands in the air and out of breath from her short trot from the dirt road to the schoolhouse. Full of pep, like always. Miss Boland's tongue was never depressed.

Miss Kelly smiled. "We can't guess."

"And I'll tell you all about it," panted Miss Boland, "soon as I catch my second wind."

Soup nudged me. "Something's up."

6

"How can you tell?" I whispered.

"Rob, I've seen Miss Boland a bit churned up before, but today I'd say her face is a shade pinker."

Soup was right. Miss Boland's chubby cheeks were pink and puffing, sort of like a big whistle that wanted to blow.

"Well," said Miss Kelly, "please don't keep us all in suspense. What's your exciting news?"

Listing heavily into the chair behind Miss Kelly's desk, Miss Boland fanned her cherry-pie face with a white hanky. She helped herself to a full breath and let out the air from her lungs. Then she spoke, chugging out her words as if they were all climbing uphill.

"It's the CCC. Or was."

Miss Kelly raised an eyebrow.

"I been pushing this project all winter to the school board, and now that spring's here it just might blossom," said Miss Boland.

"What might blossom?"

"Like I early said. It *used* to be called the CCC, the Children's Costume Contest."

Miss Kelly nodded. "We tried that two years ago, or three, but it rained so hard that it was a washout. In more ways than one. Few participated."

Miss Boland lifted a chubby finger to point at our

ceiling, which made me wonder if there was a leak in the school roof. But no, only an idea.

"Ah!" said Miss Boland. "Hardly *anyone* participated. And I'll tell you why. One, the weather. Two, we didn't get our handbills printed and passed out in time. And three, the contest was only for tots."

"You've made some changes," said Miss Kelly, "I presume."

"Right!" Miss Boland smacked her own hand with her own fist. "This year, by the golly, we're going to open the contest to everyone in town. Every man, woman, kid, dog, cat, and grandmother."

"Splendid," said Miss Kelly. "And who, may I ask, prompted so drastic a change? As if I didn't know."

"I did," said Miss Boland. "A couple of months back, remember the evening that you and I went to the picture show?"

Miss Kelly nodded. "Bank Night."

"Well, we didn't win the bank, but that was the night they showed a travelogue about New Orleans and that parade, or whatever it was."

"I recall," Miss Kelly said.

"Nobody really *saw* that little film except *me*. Because most folks were sitting in their seats thinking about Bank Night and all the loot they might rake in. But I saw it."

"And?"

"That," said Miss Boland, "is what our town needs this spring, to wake us all up. A real live whoop-de-do."

"A costume parade. Well," said Miss Kelly, "I bet you could get all the merchants behind it. If it will bring people into town."

"Check." Miss Boland jumped to her feet, her big white shoes clumping to and fro in front of our blackboard. "Not a CCC, not just a costume contest for kids, but a great big feast and festival for the whole town."

Miss Kelly smiled. "It could be fun."

"You're darn right," said Miss Boland as she almost defied gravity and leaped into the air with a little hop. "We'll show those people down in New Orleans. Because we're going to throw the biggest VMG that anybody ever saw."

"VMG?" asked Miss Kelly. "Whatever in the world is that?"

Miss Boland smiled. "Vermont Mardy Grah."

TWO

I stood in line.

Like always, we were standing in single file, ready to be dismissed from school. Before leaving, we all shook hands with our teacher, one by one.

"Good night, Miss Kelly," said Soup.

"Good night, Luther."

"Good night, Miss Kelly," I said.

"Good night, Robert."

Then I heard another kid wish a good night to Miss Kelly; but before I heard our teacher say "Good night, Janice," I was already exploding out the door at full throttle. Up ahead, Soup was chasing Ally Tidwell and Rolly McGraw. And then it happened. Somebody spoke my name.

"Rob?"

It wasn't Janice.

I stopped; pulled up short with both sneakers and turned to face the person who, only by practically whispering my name, could promote my entire body and soul to digress into an almost critical glandular condition.

Her name was Norma Jean Bissell.

Of this one fact I was dead sure, because I silently said her name about one hundred times each day. I mentioned her in my prayers. And in my dreams. Plus during my morning chores when I slopped the pigs. I could see her face in the stars, in mud puddles; even in the cracks of plaster on the ceiling over my bed. To me, the English alphabet was comprised of only sixteen letters, including a few repeats.

They spelled NORMA JEAN BISSELL, who

was now saying, "Rob, my books are so *heavy*."

Flexing the mighty muscle of my arm, a bicep that nearly approached the size of a unripe grape (but not as hard), I swept up *Hewlitt's Pictorial Geography* along with *Zimmer's Long Division* as well as *The Open Door to Spelling.*

I inhaled her.

Norma Jean Bissell seemed to emit a fragrance all her own, somewhere between Constance and honeysuckle. I wasn't too sure about the honeysuckle part, but I was sure about how Constance smelled, because I slept with her. She curled up in a shoebox that said *Red Cross* on it, under my bed.

Once in while, Constance would croak in the night, as all toads do. Distressed, perhaps, that I was dreaming not of her but of the fair Miss Bissell.

"Come on," I said to Norma Jean, "let's run."

"Why do we have to run?"

"Exercise," I said.

What I didn't want to tell her was that I had casually looked over my shoulder and had heard the thundering hoofs of Janice Ricker galloping my way. To get myself crushed like a cider apple by Janice was sorry enough. But to have Norma Jean Bissell stand around while Janice punched me to a pulp was hardly heroic.

13

"Let's go," I said, my voice climbing an octave or two with every phrase, "I'll race you to the county line."

"But that's three miles out of town."

Norma Jean didn't seem to want to hustle at all. Maybe she never ran. In school she always looked like she was going to a birthday party. She looked *new*. Compared with her, both Soup and I look *used*. Sort of third-hand. Norma Jean Bissell appeared each morning as though she'd just been starched and ironed.

Even now, at the end of a hot school day, she looked more crisp than a Christmas present.

"I never run," she said.

"Why not?"

"It isn't ladylike."

Janice was cantering closer and closer, and *she* didn't look very ladylike either. In fact, she looked ready to beat up Tarzan. And then eat all his apes. Raw.

"It's spring!" I yelled to Norma Jean, grabbing her hand and yanking her at least into low gear. It wasn't fast enough. I yanked harder. We trotted a bit faster, and I continued to bestow a tender tug at every step.

Closing my eyes, I saw the face of Janice Riker; once more whispering those three little words that mean so much: "I'll get you."

Janice had *gotten* me before. Many times. Last week

14

she'd tied me to a tree, belly to bark, loosed my belt, and filled my underpants with wet sawdust from Mr. Gilby's icehouse.

It wasn't all sawdust. Some of it was ice.

Before that, Janice had locked one arm around my neck and the other around Soup's neck and clanged our heads together, like gongs. A year ago, she had chewed half a hubcap off my coaster wagon. And every fall she'd crack hickory nuts with her teeth, throw away the nutmeats, and eat the shells.

The Riker family should have put up a sign in their front yard that warned: BEWARE OF THE KID.

Small wonder that I was now dragging Norma Jean Bissell up and over the high wall that ran behind Mrs. Ramsey's Hat Shoppe.

Everyone in town claimed that Sheila Ramsey was a bit funny between the ears. She said she never drank any hard beverages. Maybe so, yet Mrs. Ramsey sure did fall down a lot. But that, according to *her* side of the story, was because her foot kept going to sleep. Even when she was walking through town.

"Hey, you kids!"

Norma Jean Bissell and I were up on top of Mrs. Ramsey's wall, which measured near to six feet high. I looked around and saw the owner of that wall and she didn't look too overjoyed at the fact we were up there. Mrs. Ramsey glared at us from her back porch.

On the other side of the wall, charging up the alley in our direction, came Janice; her chunky legs shifting into high gear, her skull lowered like a Cape Buffalo.

"Get down!" commanded Mrs. Ramsey.

"Yes'm," I told her. "But we can't right now."

"Why not?"

"I . . . want to buy Norma Jean a hat. But all I've got is twenty-three cents, and it's home in my pig bank."

Mrs. Ramsey looked a mite displeasured. She was not, apparently, interested in enlarging her clientele to include twenty-three-cent customers. Seeing as some of her hats for ladies sold for as high as five dollars.

I'd heard that Mrs. Ramsey hand-made all the hats she sold. You'd see plenty in her store window. All of them sat on a head, a woman's head that had a hat but no body.

"Get smart with *me*, will you?"

Mrs. Ramsey looked around for something to throw. And found it. Picking up one of her extra heads (this one with no hat on it) she threw it at me and at Norma Jean Bissell.

The head missed.

I saw its blank expression go flying by, between us.

16

Sure is funny to see a woman's head sail through the air. Over the wall it flew.

So, after that was when Norma Jean and I made our hurried apologies to Mrs. Ramsey, climbed down from her wall, and walked casually home. It sure turned out to be a nifty afternoon.

The part that I enjoyed most was watching Mrs. Ramsey's head hit Janice's.

THREE

Miss Kelly tapped her ruler.

"Class," she said, "I have an exciting surprise for all of us this morning."

We leaned forward on our benches, because not too many of us were opposed to surprises.

"A new family has moved to town, which means that our school will be adding a new student to its roll . . . Beverly Bean."

The girls all clapped their hands. One more gal on *their* side, I was thinking. And so were they. Miss Kelly looked out the window. And, for some reason, the expression on her face shifted from anticipation to amazement.

In walked a *boy*.

Picking up a sheet of paper, that looked like a letter, which had been lying on her desk, Miss Kelly seemed somewhat confused. "There must be some mistake," she said.

Behind the new boy marched his father and mother. All three of them smiled. The new kid's smile seemed, to me, a bit hesitant.

"Miss Kelly?" asked the father.

"Yes?"

"How do," he said in a slow and friendly voice that seemed to be drawling every word. "Mah name is Shirley Bean, and this here is mah wife, Bruce. Charmed to make your acquaintance."

Miss Kelly, somewhat shaken, shook hands with Mr. Shirley Bean and Mrs. Bruce Bean. I couldn't believe my

20

own ears. Shirley? Bruce? No wonder they named their son Beverly. The poor kid looked like he was fixing to die of fright. He was so slicked up in clean clothes that he didn't look much like a kid. More like a flower.

Mr. Shirley Bean beamed a broad smile at all of us, and spoke: "We just moved up here to Vermont from Macon, Georgia, and ah'm with the paper company here in town. Ah s'pect we're fixin' to stay."

"Welcome," Miss Kelly managed to say.

"And," said Mr. Bean, "as Beverly's daddy, ah just know our little ol' boy here is gonna take to school real good."

Eddy Tacker made a face. Next to Janice, Eddy was the toughest kid in the school; he had a fist that was near twice as hard as a wrecking ball.

Mrs. Bruce Bean placed her hands protectively on her son's skinny shoulders and then bent over to kiss his cheek. I sort of felt sorry for little ol' Beverly. He sure didn't appear to be overjoyed. The poor kid was wearing a *necktie*. And it wasn't even Sunday.

Right then, as Miss Kelly was busy talking to Mr. and Mrs. Bean, I could hear whispering. Just about every kid in the room was mumbling "Beverly" and trying to force a straight face.

21

"Best we be going," said Mrs. Bean. "You be a good boy, Beverly, you hear? And ah know you're fixin' to do just what Miss Kelly tells you."

Mr. and Mrs. Bean departed.

Beverly, led by Miss Kelly, was seated all by himself on a bench next to Soup and me. He sure was off to a rotten run of luck. Right behind him sat Eddy Tacker.

Last year, I had to sit in front of Eddy, and it wasn't much of a treat. Oh, it was fun—if you like getting the back of your head snapped with a rubber band. Or getting a jab with a pin, farther south.

From the corner of my eye, I saw good old Eddy fumble in his pocket. Beverly Bean wasn't due for a picnic.

"Isn't it nice," said Miss Kelly, "to have a new student in our school?"

We all dutifully moaned how nice it was.

I yawned, looking around the room at all the faces. And then I got one of the shocks of my life. Norma Jean Bissell was looking at Beverly Bean with the same expression that Soup said I wore whenever I looked at *her*.

Soup noticed it, too.

"Rob," he whispered, "guess who's starting to look over yonder at dear little Beverly as if he was cookies?"

22

I didn't have to ask Soup who it was, yet he told me anyhow.

"Norma Jean Bissell."

Beverly Bean sat twice as quiet as a mouse, and didn't even twitch an itch. Or move a muscle. He probably didn't, I was trying to laugh to myself, even have a muscle to move. They sure must have had some odd folks down in Macon, Georgia. A man named Shirley? His wife, Bruce? And, to top it all off, they curse their son with a sugarfoot handle like Beverly.

Just when I was expecting that Eddy would give old Beverly a rubbery snap on the ear, I saw something else. Beverly Bean seemed to notice Norma Jean Bissell.

Then he *winked* at her!

"Georgia," said Miss Kelly, her pointer tapping our big map of the United States, "is here. See? Just north of this peninsula state we studied yesterday, which was—"

"Pittsburgh," said Janice.

Miss Kelly sighed. "My," she said, "I guess the excitement of welcoming a new scholar, not to mention a new family to our town, has us *all* a bit confused."

The day dragged on.

I thought the clock would never spin. Hour after hour, I observed Beverly Bean smiling at *my girl*. I was starting to dislike that new kid. My feelings intensified whenever

23

Norma Jean smiled back at him. It was like I was absent.
That was when I got an idea.

I already knew how Eddy Tacker felt about Norma
Jean Bissell. Sort of the way I did. So did Rolly. But it
was Eddy's feelings that I could later employ to full
advantage.

While our teacher was writing something unimportant
on the blackboard, which had to do with homework, I
pulled out a crumpled sheet of paper, carefully *printed*
some words on it, and folded it neatly. Then, while Miss
Kelly's back was still turned, I passed the note back to
Eddy.

On the outside of the note, I had written: TO
BEVERLY.

"It's for Beverly," I whispered to Eddy, "and I reckon
that it just might be from Norma Jean."

There was one custom I counted on. When notes got
passed from hand to hand in our schoolroom, it didn't
matter who the intended receiver was. Eddy Tacker
opened up every one, even when the message was private
and personal.

Today was no exception. Eddy read it.

I saw his dirty fingers unfold the note I had so slyly and
cleverly prepared. And I could tell by the way his lips
were moving that Eddy was absorbing every word.

My note was:

Dean Beverly,
   You are cute. Too bad you have to sit
in front of the kid we call Eddy Tacky.
                    Love + Kisses,
                    N. J. B.

I saw Eddy's fist crumple up the note and watched his
ruddy cheeks darken to a deeper and madder red.

My plan was working.

FOUR

We said good night to Miss Kelly.

Inside my stomach, I could still taste the big baked-
bean sandwich that Mama had packed in my lunchpail.
Maybe I'd been wrong in faking that Norma Jean note to
Beverly, knowing that Eddy would shortstop it. And

maybe I'd have to pay poor Beverly's bandage bill. It was a pity that Miss Boland wasn't around.

Out of the school we tumbled. Most of the kids headed for home, skipping off in several directions. Soup waited for me, as usual.

I waited for Eddy.

Most important of all, Eddy waited for Beverly Bean, who finally came out of the door—waiting for Norma Jean Bissell.

Eddy yelled, "Hey!"

Beverly smiled. "You mean *me?*"

"Yeah," snarled Eddy.

"What's up, Rob?" asked Soup.

"You'll see," I told him. "I got me a wild hunch that Eddy's got it in for Beverly."

"So soon?"

I nodded.

"Hey!" said Eddy. "You're the *new* kid."

Beverly Bean smiled. He still looked on the shy side to me. I was hoping Eddy wouldn't muss him up too badly. Yet, if he did, it would serve that Georgia boy right—for throwing a wink at *my girl.*

"Watch this," I told Soup.

I saw Eddy approach poor Beverly. And then I noticed that the new kid gently nudged Norma Jean to one side,

28

as if to place himself between her and the oncoming Eddy Tacker. Who did that new kid think he was, Ivanhoe?

"This'll be good," I told Soup.

"Or bad," Soup said.

"I read it," Eddy grunted.

"Read what?" asked Norma Jean.

Reaching into his pocket, Eddy pulled out the note that I had printed in class and passed back.

"Right here," Eddy said hotly.

I started to wonder if good old Eddy Tacker was going to take a swing at Norma Jean. If he did, I sure wasn't going to stand there and watch. Yet the idea of having to front up to Eddy Tacker wasn't too appealing. I hate pain.

"I'm real mad," Eddy said.

Norma Jean asked, "What over?"

"As if you didn't know."

Eddy Tacker's hands doubled into fists.

But then up spoke the new kid. His voice was real soft and slow. He sure sounded like a Beverly. "May I please see the note?"

"No," Eddie said, stuffing the note back into his pocket.

"I didn't write that," said Norma Jean.

"Nor did I," said Beverly.

"You're a liar," Eddy said, looking Norma Jean Bissell right in the eye.

"Now you behave," said Beverly Bean. "On account that a gentleman doesn't up and sass a lady."

Boy, I thought, that poor skinny Beverly is just about begging to go visit his dentist.

"This is all quite silly," said Norma Jean. "Eddy, how come you're always acting so ornery?"

"Hush up," said Eddy Tacker.

"Say," drawled Beverly, "I'd say you ought to up and apologize to this here little gal for talking to her thataway."

Eddy snickered. His hand covered his mouth for a moment and then returned to being a fist. "Kid," said Eddy, "you just don't *look* funny. You even *talk* funny."

Stepping forward, Eddy shot out his hand, giving Beverly Bean's shoulder a solid push.

"Hey! You wanna fight?" Eddy sneered.

"Not really."

"Scared?"

"No," said Beverly.

"Hah. I bet you got a yellow belly."

"Perhaps. But at least I don't have a loud mouth and rude manners."

That was when Eddy's hand struck like a snake. He reached out and yanked off Beverly's bow tie. It was the clip-on kind that I'd seen one time down at the drygoods store.

And then Eddy stomped on it.

"Now," said Beverly, "that was a little ol' mistake."

"Yeah? Well, sissy pants, I hope you got your sweet self ready for a lot more."

Reaching forward, Eddy grabbed the front of Beverly's shirt with one hand, drawing back his other hand into a hard fist. Then he swung.

But the punch never landed.

Beverly Bean grabbed Eddy's hair, squatted down real low, kicked Eddy's stomach with both feet; then shot him, rump over reason, and into the dirt.

Eddy was stunned.

Before he could get up, Beverly went over and sat on his backside, and neatly bent up one of Eddy's beefy arms so he could near scratch the back of his dirty neck.

"Allow me," said Beverly in his soft, down South voice, "to introduce myself. Bean's the name. And if 'n you s'pect we might be friends, I s'pose you can call me Bev."

"Go to heck," grunted Eddy.

Beverly Bean tightened his one-handed grip on Eddy's wrist so that Eddy's face got busy eating topsoil.

"Wow," I said.

And so did Soup.

We'd never seen anybody, except Janice, make old Eddy Tacker chew dirt. Eddy *was* the second toughest kid in the school. Now he had just slipped down to third.

"Get up, please," said Beverly Bean. "You'll soil your clothes. And would you mind fetching me my tie?"

It was some sight to see.

There was Eddy Tacker, bending over. He picked up the bow tie and fetched it back to its owner. Eddy even brushed the dirt off it.

Soup and I talked about the new kid all the way home, and how he'd given Tacker a lesson in gentlemanly behavior.

"Miss Kelly was right," said Soup.

"About what?"

"She always says manners help to build manhood."

"I don't guess Miss Kelly was wrong on that score," I told Soup.

"Ya know, Rob, she tells us a whole batch of useful stuff. So we best listen up when she tells us things. But there's one thing she didn't tell you or me or Eddy. And it's a simple rule I intend to remember."

"What's that?" I asked him.

"Never," said Soup, "pick on any boy named *Beverly*."

FIVE

"Ouch," I said.

Soup asked, *"Now* what's the matter?"

"There's a pebble in my sneaker."

We stood on Maple Street, in town; each of us holding a fat packet of handbills that Miss Boland had brought to school, earlier today, and requested that we all distribute.

According to Miss Boland's plan, each pair of kids had been assigned to cover one entire street, making sure that a handbill was stuck into each front door. I'd already read the leaflet several times over; but, untying the knot in my shoelace, I scanned it again:

```
┌─────────────────────────────────────────────┐
│                                             │
│         VERMONT MARDY GRAH                   │
│         ☆  June 10  ☆                        │
│      Come early! Wear a costume!             │
│                                             │
│      Plenty of ice cream, root beer, pretzels, │
│      cotton candy, hotdogs, and mustard!     │
│         Bring the whole family!              │
│        Bargains in every store in town!      │
│   Band concert in the park. And a square dance, │
│      providing the heavens don't weather.    │
│                                             │
│   Big prize for the most unusual costume!!!  │
│                                             │
└─────────────────────────────────────────────┘
```

"Soup?"

Soup sighed. "Yeah—"

"What do you think the prize will be?"

"Maybe," said Soup, "it'll be a pony."

"Honest?"

"Naw."

"Then what'll it be?" Turning my sneaker upside down, I returned the pebble to its planet.

"It might be a hundred dollars."

"Wow," I said.

"And fifty cents," said Soup. "But unless you hurry up so we can sow these here handbills, the tenth of June will be come and gone."

I tied my sneaker lace. "Okay," I said, picking up my stack of leaflets, "I'm ready to keep going."

"Thank gosh."

Soup covered one side of Maple Street while I ran up to front doors on the other. It was sort of fun at first. Yet I could see that my partner, Luther Wesley Vinson, was growing a trifle bored. Work never mixed too well with Soup.

Across the street, I saw Soup sitting down on the bench just outside Mrs. Blalock's white picket fence. So I trotted across the street to learn his thoughts.

"There ought to be an easier way," Soup said.

"You're right," I told him.

"Maple Street runs from one end of town," said Soup, "clear to the other."

"It could take us forever."

"If we were getting paid *wages* for all this delivering, then it might be a whole different story."

"All we get," I said, "is a coupon for one free scoop of ice cream and a free hotdog."

"Trouble with Maple Street," said Soup, "is that all the houses are set back too far from the road."

"Right," I said. "And no roadside mailboxes, like out where *we* live."

"Rob," said Soup, "if we could just noodle up a way to

get all the folks who live here on Maple Street to walk out of their houses—"

"Then," I said, "we'd just stroll along and hand them the leaflets, easy as pie, and we'd be through in jig time. They'd all come to us."

"With hardly any *work*," said Soup, as if he'd just spoken a dirty word. And wanted to spit.

"All we have to do, Soup, is figure out a way to lure folks outdoors, so they'll march down to the curb."

Soup nodded, scratching his head.

"Well," I asked Soup, "what'll bring 'em out?"

Soup smiled. "A *fire*."

"No," I said.

This was one of Soup's many suggestions with which I wasn't aiming to string along. It sure didn't make any sense to burn down the entire town so that a couple of lazy loafers could pass out leaflets with less strain.

"It wouldn't have to be a *big* fire," Soup said.

I shook my head. "No, not even a little fire. Not one spark."

"Okay," said Soup. "You got any matches?"

"Nope. You?"

Soup searched his pockets. "Nary a one."

I puffed out a sigh of deep relief. "Then I don't guess we'll strike up much of a flame."

"Rob, we don't actual *need* a fire."

"What *do* we need?"

Soup grinned. "A fire *whistle*."

I noticed right then that Soup was looking over his shoulder, back toward town, to where our one-and-only fire station was located. Inside was a red fire truck. But up on the roof was the loudest red whistle in three counties.

"I won't do it, Soup."

"Do what?"

"Blow the fire whistle."

"Maybe a fire's not such a *hot* idea," said Soup.

"No," I said. "It sure isn't."

"But it wouldn't hurt to walk down to the firehouse and just *look*, would it?"

I sighed. "I suppose not."

How, minutes later, I found myself up on the steep roof of the fire station, I will never truly know. I was crawling up the slanted roof, inching closer and closer to a red whistle that was bigger than a rain barrel. I sort of had a hanker to see it up close. But maybe not *this* close.

Soup was underneath me, pushing up on the soles of my feet, so I wouldn't slip and slide down the shingles.

"Soup?"

"Quiet," Soup hissed at me. "There's three or four firemen down there, playing cards."

"Okay," I said. "We *saw* the whistle. Now what?"

"Remember," warned Soup in a whisper, "whatever else you do, promise me you *won't* sound the alarm."

I knew I sure wasn't doing that.

"Look close, Rob."

"At what?"

"Take a look at the whistle," said Soup, "and see if maybe there's some special little button you can press that's marked Maple Street."

"Huh?"

"See that long arm with the chain hanging down from the whistle? To your right."

"Yup, I see it."

"Okay, look on top of that arm."

"An alarm button for Maple Street wouldn't be up on that arm, Soup. Would it?"

Soup said, "Touch it and see. But don't pull."

For some dumb reason I lightly rested my hands on the iron arm that protruded from the big red barrel. And that was when good old Luther Vison did what I never expected him to do.

Soup let go of my feet.

As I started to slide, in that one split second, there was only one thing to hang on to. So I grabbed it as I fell. It was the long iron arm of the fire whistle.

BBRRRAAAAMMMMM! . . .

I thought my heart was going to blow up. Or both ears explode. It was like the dead center of a war. Below me, I saw Soup skin down the ladder. That was when I let loose, tumbled, and fell.

Two men ran outside. One grabbed Soup, the other grabbed me; and they both gave us one merry hiding and it hurt like fury. Firemen have hard hands. Not even my father could spank that heavy. But as Soup and I went limping away from the firehouse, I saw that my pal was smiling. His unusual powers of recovery were taking over.

"Rob," said Soup, "it really worked. Look at all those people rushing out their front doors."

Later on, as we passed out our handbills to the curious residents of Maple Street who'd popped outdoors, Soup actually had the nerve to say something:

"All part of the Mardy Grah, folks."

I couldn't quite understand how Soup could sound so joyful. My butt was still burning.

"Hey," I said, as we passed out the last handbill to the last citizen who we then left still looking for a fire, "that licking we got at the firehouse wasn't too much fun. And look at the trouble you got us into."

"Yeah," said Soup, "but I sure got us out of work."

SIX

"Gotcha," growled Janice.

It was noon at school. We'd all pigged down our lunches and were spending the rest of our hour (fifty-nine minutes) behind the school, playing Janice Riker's favorite game, the one she had invented.

She called it Tackle Tag.

Janice had just tackled Rolly McGraw, who was a lot tougher than I was, and was happily burying old Rolly's face into the Vermont topsoil.

"I give," Rolly was yelping.

Earlier in the day, Miss Kelly had taught us a few facts about Mr. Thomas Alva Edison, who was one of America's greatest inventors.

"Get off," Rolly screamed at Janice.

At the moment, as she (plus a few others) was still astride Rolly's back, Janice Riker didn't remind me a whole lot of Mr. Edison. And I had a hunch that Rolly was not about to celebrate the fact that Janice had invented Tackle Tag.

"Okay," said Janice, as she finally dismounted from Rolly, "*now* who's going to be It?"

No one volunteered.

Janice glowered at Soup and he took a cautious step backward. Then she looked at Eddy Tacker, Ally Tidwell, and finally at me. I saw Soup pointing my way, the rat.

"Rob Peck is It," said Janice with a smirk.

Miss Kelly always told us how lucky were were to live in a democracy, even though most of us Vermonters were Republicans. However, our playground was *not* a democracy. In no way.

Janice was King, Queen, and Goddess . . . not to mention two more. Umpire and Referee.

Soup nudged me. "Go ahead, Rob. You haven't been It yet. So you're next."

"Yeah," snarled Janice. "You ain't been."

"I was It yesterday," I told her.

"That don't count," said Janice. Soup smiled, and I could have belted him.

The rules of Tackle Tag were not found in rule books. They were formed on the spot by Janice Riker.

"Rob's It," said Soup.

Janice nodded, making it official.

Tackle Tag wasn't played the way you'd play Tag the regular way. In a regular game of Tag, the It person chased everybody until someone was caught. Janice's rules were the complete opposite. She said that in Tackle Tag, the It got chased by everybody.

It wasn't a whole lot of fun for the It kid, as Rolly's obvious lumps and bruises attested.

Janice looked at me. "Ready?"

I sighed. "Ready."

"Go!"

I ran, first dodging Soup and Rolly (he was easy because he was still limping), and then Ally Tidwell. After that, I head-faked Paul Leitz and Seaborn Goebel.

"Get'im!" Janice was bellowing.

As I ducked, Soup crashed into Ally and I saw them both tumble in a heap. Janice was hot on my trail, yet I managed to elude her every charge. Not that I'm a swift runner or anything close to it. But whenever Janice Riker is bearing down on me, I run for my life. She was a kid who inspired us all.

Janice appeared to be more than just a little out of breath. "Time out," she was gasping.

Soup looked at Janice. "Who says?"

"Me," puffed Janice. "I can call a time out whenever I favor to, because I'm the umpire."

Rolly, who had pulled up short just behind me, whispered into my ear. "Umpire? A better word for her would be *vampire*."

Glancing at Janice, I giggled. This turned out to be my major mistake of the month.

Diving my way, Janice yelled "Time *in!*"

I darted.

This was no time to place myself at the very bottom of a hog pile of kids, with Janice Riker on top as the heaviest hog.

Not that I'm any champion player, but one thing I've observed is this. Whenever you play Tackle Tag, it's the It that always loses and the Janice who always wins.

As I was now busily running and dodging the rest of the gang, I kept an ear cocked for any telltale rumbles of danger . . . mainly the approaching thunder of Janice's hoofs. But it didn't look good.

I was now surrounded on three sides by humans; on the fourth, by Janice Riker.

Maybe my only chance, I told myself, is to outsmart her. Janice was heavy on muscle but a bit feathery of brain. Soup always claimed that the hardest five years of Janice's education had been first grade.

Yet I had to give old Janice credit. Whenever we'd play Tackle Tag, she had repeatedly enforced her rule that the inventor of the game never had to be It.

Soup grabbed at me, and missed.

Right then, I had a brainstorm. It was as if a shining light suddenly pierced the darkness of my despair. Inspiration hit me.

"Hey!" I yelled. "Who's the inventor of Tackle Tag?"

"Me," snorted Janice. "I'm it."

I stopped running. "Hear that, everybody? Janice just said that she was It."

Janice looked blank. "Huh?"

"You heard it," I hollered. Then I stared Rolly McGraw right in the eye, and said "Janice says she's It. Are *you* gonna argue with *Janice*?"

"Not me," said Rolly.

Janice Riker's face turned into one big puzzle. I could detect in a second that she was thinking. This, for me, was a good sign. It meant hope instead of a hospital.

"You win, Janice," I yelled. "You're *It!*"

"Wait," Janice was panting.

Yet it was no use. They all tackled Janice. No, that's not quite right. They *tried* to.

Rolly grabbed her left leg and Ally her right. Soup dived for her head, along with Seaborn and Paul and Eddy Tacker. They all looked like ripe tomatoes splattering against a brick wall. I don't recall how tough Mr. Thomas Edison was, but then I saw that Janice Riker was one tough inventor.

From the expression on Janice's face, I could tell that she was trying her level best to think up a new rule. Then I saw her smile. That, I thought, was an evil omen.

"Get her down!" yelled Soup.

Yet it was of little use. Janice stumbled forward, still on her feet, with Seaborn, Paul, Rolly, Eddy and Ally clinging to her like a litter of opossums. I don't know how she did it, but she did. No one would believe what I saw.

With a mighty grunt, Janice lurched from low gear into high, heading for her goal. Twenty feet ahead of her was the playground mud puddle.

Then fifteen feet. Now ten. Five, four, three, two, one . . .

"No," screamed Soup.

I could only watch with horror, as I was too winded from my turn at being It to pitch in.

Well, they finally got Janice down. But they all went with her. Janice crash-landed at the exact center of the puddle, right where she knew the mud was the deepest. And gloppiest.

Sppllaaaattttt.

Mud flew everywhere; and it sure was hard, from that moment on, to tell who was who. To me, it sort of looked as though It had somehow tackled everyone else. Except me. There didn't seem to be too much mud left in the puddle. A lot of it was in the air. But most of it now frosted Ally, Eddy, Seaborn, Rolly, and Paul.

Janice, surprisingly enough, seemed to be the cleanest. In addition, she was also the first kid to stand up. For some reason, she seemed to be taller than usual. Then I figured out why.

She was standing on Soup.

SEVEN

It was Saturday.

Early, even before my morning chores were over, Soup came to whack our kitchen door. He had a fishpole in one hand and a brown paper bag under his other arm.

"Are you two boys going fishing?" Aunt Carrie asked.

Soup said, "Yes'm, we sure are."

"Where?"

Aunt Carrie and Mama had to be the two most curious people on this earth; with maybe Mrs. Vinson, Soup's ma, coming in a close third. Those three ladies must stay up all night in order to dream up so many useless questions.

"Down to Putt's Crick," said Soup.

Mama asked, "Near the pond?"

I said, "Yes."

But then Soup shot me a quick look before adding, "Not too near."

Aunt Carrie said, "I heard tell the water's always deep in that crick pond this time of year. Isn't it?"

"Not where *we* go," said Soup. "We're not after the big fish, and all the real whoppers are up in the pond. We're just after a few crap."

"Carp," said Mama, using the word that Miss Kelly insisted we use in the schoolroom. I never understood why. Just about every man or boy in town who ever fished Putt's Crick called 'em *crappies*.

They were only *carp* in books.

"Carp," said Soup.

Mama smiled, maybe not knowing that Luther Vinson was straining to make an impression—anything to skirt the subject of how deep was Putt's Crick.

"When will you boys be back?" asked Mama.

"About an hour," I said, prior to thinking.

Aunt Carrie snorted. "It takes an hour to hike that far. How far is it?"

"Near a mile," said Soup.

Mama said, "Rob, do you want me to pack you up a noon meal?"

I told her that I'd already put my lunch up. It was outside in a paper sack. All I'd packed was one of her small jars of pickles because Soup said he'd bring us some sandwiches.

"Are you sure," Aunt Carrie spoke up, "you boys will be all right?"

"Yes'm," said Soup.

"When you're way back in those woods," Mama asked, "who'd ever be able to hear you if you called for help?"

"We don't call," I said.

Soup said, "It might scare the fish."

"The two of you," said Mama, "off in the middle of nowhere."

"Maybe," said Aunt Carrie, "I best go along with them. In case they fall in."

A big help she'd be, I thought. Aunt Carrie couldn't as much as swim one stroke. As a fisherman, Aunt Carrie was just one thing—a sinker.

"If the two of you wander off," said Mama, "or get lost, how would we *ever* find you?"

"We won't," said Soup.

"All this worry," Mama said, "just to hook a crap."

"Carp," said Aunt Carrie.

"How well can you swim, Luther?" asked Mama.

"Real good," Soup answered back.

This was sort of true. Soup could stroke out a dog paddle a bit faster than I could. Neither of us was ready to be Tarzan.

"Just be careful," warned Mama.

"Yes'm," said Soup. "We will. Let's go, Rob."

I asked Soup if he'd dug up the worms.

"Yup."

Aunt Carrie looked around. "Where are they?"

"In the bag," said Soup, "with my lunch."

Mama and Aunt Carrie made faces, which meant that one of them just might be cranking up a lecture on worms or germs. Maybe both.

"Be sure," said Mama, "that both of you wash your hands before you touch your food. Promise?"

"Yes," I said, escaping through the screen door and off the porch, carrying my pole and my bag with the jar of pickles in it.

Soup and I ran most of the way, heading straight for Putt's Pond, the place where the water was deepest. And, we hoped, the fish were the biggest.

After about three hours without a bite, Soup said,

"Maybe the crappies aren't hungry. But I sure am. Let's eat."

Quickly, I dipped both hands into the water, pretending to wash. After all, I'd promised Mama. Soup then opened up his brown bag and yanked something out.

Pickles!

"What kind of sandwiches did you pack, Rob?"

Saying nothing, I just pulled out *my* jar of pickles. We sort of sat there, on the grass of the crick bank, looking at two jars of pickles; each of us wearing half a smile.

"Good," said Soup. "Anyhow, I always did favor pickles ahead of peanut butter. Don't you?"

"Sure," I said. "Leastwise, I never ate a pickle that stuck in my mouth and wouldn't gulp down."

Soup and I each ate a pickle. Then another. The second one didn't seem to taste as good as the first. And my third pickle tasted worse. Even more sour than my stomach. So I tried one of Soup's pickles and he switched over to one of mine.

"Rob, we gotta think."

"About what?" I asked Soup.

"We best give some thought as to what we're going to dress up as. Miss Boland's big Vermont Mardy Grah, or whatever it's called, is next Saturday."

"Yeah," I said. "A week off. I already know what Janice

Riker's going to be. I heard her tell she's fixing to be a gorilla."

Soup laughed. "Smart. Because if old Janice is a gorilla, she won't need a costume."

I choked on a pickle.

"Rob, old top, we gotta dream up outfits for ourselves that'll really pop the eyes of those judges."

"Sure," I said. "But like *what?*"

"*What* may not," said Soup, between bites of his fifth pickle, "be as important as *how.*"

I waited for Soup to swallow his half-chewed pickle and say more.

"The way I figure it," said Soup, "the secret is *how* we make our big entrance. So we look strange, but make our entrance even stranger."

Soup looked back over his shoulder at the pasture. I saw his face light up and his arm point. So I looked, too. All I saw was one animal, leaning against the fence.

It was Mrs. McGee's mule, Margaret.

"There's our answer," said Soup.

I said, "You mean we'll dress up as *Margaret?*"

"Right. Because everybody in town will go as a single something," said Soup. "So you and I'll go double, and win."

"And split the prize, fifty-fifty."

"Sure," said Soup. "Half for me and half for Margaret."

I stared at him. "We're going as a *mule?*"

Soup winked. "Right, and that's the beauty of it. Because nobody else in town will have the brains to dream up such an idea. Two of us in *one* costume. Rob, that old prize is just about already in our pockets."

"Says you."

"All we have to do now," said Soup, "is study Margaret and then gussy up to look like her twin sister. For you, that ought to be easy. It'll be a lot harder for me."

I looked at Margaret. "You know, it just might work. Soup, how did you ever think up such a wild idea?"

Soup grinned. "I'm always inspired by pickles."

EIGHT

We didn't hook any crappies.

For most of the afternoon, Soup and I just sort of lay in the shade, throwing a pebble or two into the pond. And munching pickles.

"I'm thirsty," I finally said.

"Here," said Soup, passing me his jar. "Treat yourself to a good healthy swig of pickle juice."

On a hot day, my favorite drink is iced tea with some lemon and sugar in it. And I right then decided, after one swallow, my least favorite beverage was warm pickle juice. It was almost as tasty as battery acid. To me, it tasted anything but inspirational.

"I wonder what time it's getting to be."

"Early," said Soup.

"Best I be at the barn by chore time, or heck won't hold it. Whenever I get home too late and find Aunt Carrie milking, I'm in deep and dire trouble."

"Same for me," said Soup. "So maybe we best think about bounding for home."

"Okay," I said.

"However," said Soup, "let's sort of saunter by the dump on the way back. Just to see what we can dig up for our mule costume."

"Suits me," I said, laughing.

"Want another pickle, Rob?"

"Well," I said, "maybe one more. Just so's we don't have to tote home jars with only one pickle left in each."

Soup and I ate our last two pickles, but it took us about half an hour to do it. We chewed as we walked toward the dump; our fishpoles were over our shoulders, our bare feet kicking trails like fishbones into the dust.

"Well," said Soup, "here we are."

Looking at all the piles of junk at the dump, I sure didn't see too much that reminded me a whole lot of Margaret.

"I was sort of wishing," Soup said, "that maybe some soul in town had throwed away an old mule costume."

Nobody had.

"What'll we do, Soup?"

"Easy," said Soup. "We'll make one."

"How?"

"Well, here's an old shoebox. Over there's a half-busted deer head. Just rip off the ears."

Soup watched. With lots of yanking, I tore off the deer's ears, and Soup stuck both of them in one end of the shoebox.

"We use two buttons for eyes," Soup said, "and look over yonder. An old busted-up piano."

Using several yellowing piano keys for teeth, we suddenly had a head on our shoulders. Even though it didn't favor Margaret McGee a whole lot.

"And," said Soup, "all we do is wrap a couple of old burlap bags around our legs."

"What'll we use for a body?"

"That," said Soup, "I already figured out. Rob, how strong are you?"

I was about to say, "Real strong," but whenever I admitted it to Soup, it most usually could muddy up trouble. So I didn't say it. I kept mum.

Stepping forward, Soup felt the muscle of my arm, which I made hard to impress him.

"Wow," said Soup. "That old arm of yours is starting to swell up real mean and mighty."

"Thanks."

"Rob, I got me a hunch you're so tough that you'd be able to tote a stomach."

"A stomach full of what?"

Soup smiled. "Air. Our mule's middle won't be big. Sort of medium. And it'll be emptier than Janice's brain."

"Well," I said, "maybe I can."

"This here barrel," said Soup, "will be Margaret's body. We use more burlap for her neck, and to wrap around the barrel. Now all we need is a tail."

Bending over, I sorted through some foul-smelling trash. "Here's an old busted broom, Soup. Looks okay."

Soup frowned. "Not quite right. The bristles are too yellow. We need some sort of a doohicky that's black."

We found half a bucket of tar, but it proved to be too hardened to dip the broom bristles into.

"What we want," Soup said, "are strings."

"Long and straight?"

"Check."

"Well, I don't see anything at all."

Soup smiled. "I do."

"What?"

"Piano wire. Rob, here it all is, under our very noses, and we managed to miss it."

As I stood there in the middle of the town dump, I was wondering why Soup suddenly was so busy. One strand at a time, he tied piano wire around my waist like a belt; most of the wire hung down behind me.

"There," said Soup.

"Do I look like Margaret's tail?"

"Rob, you certain do. In so many wondrous ways."

"Yeah," I said, "but I sort of wanted to wear the head. You know, our shoebox with ears and buttons and piano keys."

Soup sighed. "We can't *both* wear a head. Yet that's not the point. Rob, how high can you kick?" All of a sudden Soup kicked his legs backward, but he didn't kick very high.

"I can kick higher," I said.

"Prove it."

That was when I kicked my legs up and bucked higher than Soup did by at least a couple of feet.

Soup said, "Okay, you win."

"I get to be the hind hoofs."

"Right," said Soup, "because it's easy to see that you're by far the best kicker."

It was folly to argue. Even earlier, when Soup had spotted Margaret and first got his costume idea, I already knew who'd march in front as the head. And who'd be the tail. Me.

"After all," said Soup, "it's sort of my turn."

"*Your* turn?"

Soup nodded. "Remember when we marched in the band? You were always in front of me, Rob. In the parade."

"I remember. That's because you got to beat our big bass drum, and be a star. All I did was carry it."

"So, it's *my* turn to be up front," said Soup. "Besides, when two people are in a mule, the one who has all the fun is the *kicker*."

"Honest?"

"Sure," said Soup. "Would I lie?"

"What do *you* do?"

"I wiggle my ears."

"You're sure all I have to do is kick?"

"Not only kick," said Soup. "You also get to do the funny part."

"Like what?"

"You swish your wire tail."

"But that's all I have to do."

"Well, one more thing. You carry something to hide the entire upper half of your body."

"What do I have to carry?"

Soup smiled. "Just the barrel."

NINE

Clink!

The sound woke me up.

Lying in bed, I heard the noise a second time. And
then again. Rolling out of bed, I went to my window,
squinting out into the moonlight.

"*Pssttt,*" whispered Soup.

There he was, with his clothes on, down on the ground and motioning for me to climb out the window and skin down the apple tree.

"Rob, get yourself dressed."

"What for? It must be near to ten o'clock."

Soup hissed, "I know that. But I heard something that ought to be fun."

"Like what?"

"I'll tell you on the way."

Why I got dressed and climbed down, I'll never know. Soup and his midnight excursions often led me to Mama's hairbrush, which she didn't use on my hair. It was the back of the brush applied to the back of me.

"Where we going?"

"You'll never guess what I heard," said Soup.

"I'll bite."

Soup flashed me a grin in the dark. "Elvina Thorpe stopped by our house with some gossip. She was talking to my mother, but I happened to overhear it all. Like a spy."

"What was it?"

"Miss Boland's got a boy friend."

"Honest?" I almost shouted.

"Quiet," warned Soup. "Or that aunt of yours will wake up."

Aunt Carrie had already commented, earlier today, when I'd tracked some harmless mud into the parlor, that what I needed was a good sound thrashing. I'd also not washed up proper, for supper, and left smudges on the kitchen towel. So I sure didn't want to wake up Aunt Carrie.

The two of us cut across the back pasture, down Harland Road, and arrived at Miss Boland's house. Most of the homes were dark. But at her house the kitchen light was burning.

"Who's her boy friend, Soup?"

"You'll see."

Creeping along the hedge behind the house, we stood up on a garbage can to peek in a back window. Sure enough, Soup was right. I saw Miss Boland with her gentleman friend.

I hoped they'd be kissing.

No such luck. Yet they sure were busy. I saw a box on the kitchen table. The man's back was to me so I couldn't see his face. Until he spun halfway around.

It was Mr. Horace Jubert.

I couldn't believe it. Miss Boland and Mr. Jubert were courting? An event like this just wasn't to be believed.

"Holy cow!" I whispered to Soup, who reached up his hand to muffle my open mouth.

"Shh!" he said to me.

The box on the table was a big one. It took near forever for them to open it up. Layer upon layer of brown paper was unfolded, and then I saw Miss Boland's eyes widen.

"Ahh," she said, smiling.

But then Mr. Jubert said something. "This here's a tomfool idea, if you ask me."

"Just you wait," Miss Boland told him as she reached both hands into the big box.

Mr. Jubert snorted with disgust as he watched our country nurse tug at something inside.

"It's perfect," Miss Boland said. "I'm so glad we ordered it." She was smiling about as wide as the rest of her.

"Humph," grunted Mr. Jubert. "I don't know why I ever let you talk me into being a part of·such a stupid contraption."

"At least you could help."

What they pulled out of the box seemed to be an almost endless gray blanket. I saw a silver zipper on one of its edges. Then out came four little black objects that looked like baby lampshades, shaped sort of like the bin of a funnel.

Mr. Jubert scowled. This was not too unusual as I

don't recall ever having seen him with any other
expression. He pointed at the four black things. "What in
Sam Hill are those?"

Miss Boland smiled. "Hoofs."

Soup looked at me with dismay, and I looked likewise
at him. What in the name of goodness, I wondered, were
these two folks up to?

Mr. Jubert did not look overjoyed. "I ought to have my
head examined," he muttered.

"Very well," said Miss Boland, "we shall now examine
your head. Here it is."

I couldn't believe what I saw her lift out of the box.
Even after I'd blinked a few times. That was when I heard
Soup whisper one little sorry word.

"No."

Miss Boland held up a mule's head.

"I can't believe it," I said.

Soup whispered, "Neither can I."

Mr. Jubert, apparently, couldn't believe it either.
Peeking over the two half-moon lenses of his wire-rim
glasses, he scowled at the mule's head that Miss Boland
was studying. "Dang it," he said. "If you think I intend to
put a ridiculous thing like that on *my* head, you got
another think coming."

Miss Boland sighed. "Now, now, Horace . . ."

"Don't you now-now *me*. I s'pose you want the whole town to call me an idiot."

"Then I'll be the head," said Miss Boland, "and you can be back in the tail."

Mr. Jubert frowned. "In the tail? What kind of a jackass do you take me for?"

Miss Boland giggled.

"Cuss it," grumbled Mr. Jubert, "you know I got me a bad back. The person in the rear's got to bend over. So I get to be the head."

"Very well, Horace." Miss Boland handed him the mule's head. "Then try it on for size."

I never thought the day (or night) would come when I'd be standing on a garbage can, in the dark, watching Mr. Horace Jubert turn himself into a mule. The mule head had a cloth neck that covered the upper part of Mr. Jubert like a gray shawl. His body was about as lean as a shovel handle. Yet the top of him sure did resemble a mule.

Soup sighed. "There goes our prize."

I figured Soup was right. Their costume sure looked to be a better mule than the stuff Soup and I had collected at the dump.

"Help me," urged Miss Boland.

We watched her struggle into the other half. It was a tight squeeze. Miss Boland should have ordered a costume for an elephant. I saw Mr. Jubert peek out from the little screen window under the chin of his mule head.

"How do I look, Horace?"

Mr. Jubert snorted. "Like a jackass."

Miss Boland finally got Mr. Jubert to try on the gray pants that would be their mule's front legs. Bit by bit and piece by piece, a lumpy mule took shape. He was in front, still wearing the head, while she was bent over in the rear.

"Well?" asked the muffled voice of Miss Boland, coming from somewhere inside the huge mass of gray bulges. "Say something, Horace."

"*Hee haw*," said Mr. Jubert.

TEN

It was Friday.

Tomorrow would be the big day. Our town's first Vermont Mardy Grah. But I wasn't feeling very joyful.

"Cheer up," said Soup.

We were on our way home from school, trying to think of another costume. Our mule couldn't compare to the expensive outfit that we'd seen through Miss Boland's back window. She and Mr. Jubert would certainly hee-haw their way into the heart of every judge.

"We don't stand a chance," I said.

75

"Never say die," said Soup.

"Well, what'll we do?"

"Climb a tree," Soup said. "Ideas come from above."

As the two of us were cutting through a patch of woods behind the paper mill, a tree wasn't too hard to locate. Less than a minute later, Soup and I straddled the biggest limb of a veteran maple, astride it as if the branch was a wooden horse.

Or a mule.

"Well," I said, "we can no longer be Margaret."

"No," said Soup. "Yet that doesn't mean that we can't noodle up something better."

"Maybe we best go to the dump and start over."

Soup was quiet.

I could tell by his expression that Luther Wesley Vinson was up a tree, yet in deep thought. I say this for my pal. Soup is no quitter.

"Hush," whispered Soup.

Then I realized why he'd said it. Somebody was shuffling through the woods. I could hear leaves rustle, then two voices, a boy's and a girl's. But who?

Soup and I hid, and waited; up among all the green maple leaves where nobody'd see us. The two people below were walking right under our tree, and then I finally saw who it was. I almost fell.

It was Beverly Bean and Norma Jean.

Darn him! Didn't that new kid know that Norma Jean Bissell was *my girl?* He didn't seem to know it. Neither did she. Because she was sort of looking at Beverly like he was a sweet roll.

The two of them were standing under the tree, facing each other, speaking softly.

"Miss Bissell, you sure are one pretty gal," I heard Beverly say.

"Why, thank you. You're so sweet."

"I can't wait until tomorrow. Can you?"

"No, I surely can't. And won't all the people be surprised when they see what we're going to be, Beverly."

"We'll just up and win for certain."

"You bet we will. My, but these books of mine are heavy. They must weigh a ton."

"Here," said Beverly Bean. "A precious little ol' thing like you ought not to have to tote her own books."

"You're so nice, Beverly. And you're such a gentleman. I declare."

I declare?

Were my ears playing tricks on me? How come Norma Jean Bissell, who was born and raised right here in Vermont, was suddenly starting to talk so slowly? And with a Georgia accent. Her voice was sounding as if she'd been weaned on nothing but jasmine and honeysuckle.

I had to admit that Beverly Bean sure was one smooth talker. Like he choked on velvet. Compared with his voice, my words sounded as if I gargled each morning with gravel and pickle juice.

Maybe, I decided, I'd gussy myself up a bit for tomorrow. Like wash, and try to comb down my hair. I sure wished I could look as well groomed as that new kid always looked. Soup once said that my hair reminded him of mad straw.

Beneath our tree, things were real silent. I couldn't see what was going on. So I leaned forward a little; and then an inch or so more, straining to catch a glimpse of whatever that Bean kid was up to with *my girl*. Darn him.

My foot slipped.

"*Ahhhhhhhhhhhhhhhh!*" I screamed.

I must have hit at least a dozen branches on the way down. Some were twigs that only felt scratchy. But others felt like I was in a fight against both Eddy Tacker and Janice Riker.

Whump!

If those branches were hard, Vermont was one heck of a lot harder. I blinked at the fireworks in front of my eyes and wondered how many bones I'd busted. Probably I'd been killed dead, had I not been a bit lucky. I landed in a thorn bush.

All I could hear was the ringing in my ears as I saw Norma Jean and Beverly go scampering off, laughing. And holding hands. They seemed to be aware of only each other.

Soup climbed down.

"Help me off with my shirt, Soup."

"Okay," he said. "What's left of it."

"My back is killing me. All smarty."

Soup laughed. "Those old thorns could monogram a marble."

"What's my back look like?"

"A row of stripes. Red on white. You sort of look like a human barber pole."

My shirt was in tatters. Mama or Aunt Carrie had just mended the elbows, too. A fresh patch on each.

"Stripes," said Soup again. He was smiling. "That's brilliant!"

I tried to get up, but one of my ankles was twisted and starting to puff up. All I could do was limp. Worse than that, I wanted to just lie down and wail. Life sure could turn rancid.

"Easy," said Soup.

He was busily jerking a few remaining thorns out of my back. And they hurt worse coming out than they had going in.

"I can't walk," I said.

"Sure you can. Just try. Nobody ever gets anywhere in the world unless they learn to hobble over pain. You want to win the big prize for the most original outfit tomorrow, don't you?"

"Yeah, but—"

"Well," said Soup, "then best we get home and start painting our costume."

"*Painting* it?"

"Right," said Soup. "I just took myself one long look at all those colorful stripes across your back, and came up with a peachy idea."

"We're going as a *peach?*"

"Nope," said Soup.

"What as?"

"You'll see, Rob, old top. My pa's got some paint in our barn. All we need to pilfer is a can of black and a can of white. To make the rows of stripes."

"We're going to be *prisoners?*"

"Better than that," said Soup.

Leaning most of the way on Soup, I limped home.

And hid my shirt in the chicken coop. In front of Mama and Aunt Carrie, I walked real normal; even though my swollen ankle throbbed like a drum. Soup trotted home and then came back with the paint, insisting that I was either tough enough to help or he'd find himself another pal, and partner.

So I helped.

We painted stripes on all our burlap bags. Then we added a few brushstrokes to our shoebox. Much of the paint was on me because I had to do most of the work.

What we finished up with was a mess that resembled neither a peach nor a prisoner. My back was smarting and my ankle hurt like heck, but at least we were finally done.

Soup inspected my paint job. "Not overly neat," he said, "but she'll probable do."

I still didn't understand what we were doing, or why. "Whatever we got," I said, "it sure doesn't look much like Margaret anymore."

"It's not supposed to," said Soup.

"Gosh, I give up. I don't guess we're going to go to the Mardy Grah as a mule. But what else can we be inside a barrel and this black and white mess of burlap?"

Soup grinned. "Rob, we're a zebra."

ELEVEN

Saturday morning arrived.

"Soup's here," I said as I saw him coming.

"Thank goodness," said Aunt Carrie. "I doubt that I could start my day's work without a glimpse of him."

Trying not to limp, yet wearing a painful face, I sneaked out the kitchen door. Soup was carrying a white sugar sack that contained some odd-looking bulges. Real strange.

"What'cha got, Soup?"

"Nothing," said Soup. "Just a little surprise. How's that bad ankle of yours?"

"Awful."

Bending over, Soup pulled up the pant leg of my faded overalls to offer his medical opinion. "Well," said Soup, "it looks about twice as fat as your good ankle. So maybe it's twice as strong. I figure you'll be able to rest weight on it."

I took a few steps. It hurt like all fury. Inside my ankle, I felt a little explosion every second, as though grenades were going off. Soup looked at me in disgust. "Girls," said Soup, "are nothing but trouble."

I wanted to tell Soup that *he* was nothing but trouble. Soup and his stupid tree climbing and his dumb zebra. The paint was still on my hands and wouldn't scrub off. Plus the fact that I could swear (and I mean *swear*) that my backside was still harboring more than one thorn.

"You're lucky, Rob."

"How come?"

"Just plain lucky," said Soup, "that ya got *me*." Then, as Soup finished saying it, he held up his mysterious sugar sack.

"Soup, I can't be in the contest. There's no way I can parade up and down Main Street in front of those judges and kick like either a mule or a zebra. Or even kick like a grasshopper."

"Okay," said Soup. "You won't have to kick."

"Kick? I can barely walk."

Soup smiled, resting his hand on my shoulder. "Rob, old top, I got it all planned out. And the good news is—you won't even have to walk *one step*."

Again he pointed at his sugar sack.

Part of Soup's good news was the fact that, minutes later, Mr. and Mrs. Vinson came by with their team and buckboard, so we all got a ride into town. Papa had to work that day, but Mama and Aunt Carrie went along, in the second seat.

Soup and I rode backward, in the tail bin, holding our (we hoped) prize-winner zebra costume on our laps. We also brought along our barrel. Everybody asked questions as to what Soup and I were intended to be, in costume. Aunt Carrie, after eying us and the barrel, guessed "Rainwater."

My ankle was still hurting. "Soup, how'll you fix it so's I don't have to walk one single step?"

"You'll find out." Soup winked.

"What's in the sack?"

85

"A surprise," said Soup. "Remember now, I'm doing all this for *you*, so act grateful."

"When we're in our zebra costume," I whispered to him, "I guess I'll get to sit down."

"Well," said Soup, "not quite. As I explained to you a while back, the day we went fishing, I figure the secret to winning the contest depends more on *how* we enter. Not so much on *what* we dress up as."

"I don't get it."

"Oh, you'll get it," Soup reassured me. "Don't worry."

I never did worry a whole lot. Hardly at all. With me, real worrying only began whenever Luther Vinson said, "Don't worry." Those two words of his were always a surefire signal for total disaster.

Soup had glued two buttons on our shoebox, for zebra eyes, had tied in the piano-key teeth with string, and had stretched on a couple of rubber bands to hold the ears in place. Yet even the black and white stripes that I'd added yesterday wouldn't convince the most imaginative judge that it looked at all like a zebra.

Yet it certainly wasn't Margaret, the mule.

"We'll enter ourselfs last," said Soup, "and that's when we make our grand impressive entrance. Believe me, Rob, we'll be the stars of the show."

"And I don't have to walk on my bad ankle."

Soup shook his head. "Don't worry."

"Why do you keep telling me not to worry? It worries me."

"Leave it to me, Rob. I got me a special kind of a brain that can always work stuff out."

My fingers stretched out and felt the sugar sack that Soup had tied up tight at its neck with a length of old clothesline. Inside the sack was something hard. Several things, made out of metal.

"I give up, Soup. What's in it?"

"The answer to our prayers. Our hopes, our dreams, and our winning the prize for the most original getup."

"I know. *Don't worry.*" My hands were wet with sweat. "Do you actually think we got a chance to win?"

"Rob, it's in the bag."

"That's what I'm afraid of."

We all arrived in town. Main Street was a mob of cars, pickup trucks, horses, wagons, and people.

The whole place was one big costume. To me, it appeared as if most everybody had opened up an attic trunk to deck out into an absurd variety of disguises. Two of the best had come as Raggedy Ann and Raggedy Andy. They were perfect. I was admiring the two of them until I heard Andy speak to Ann.

"Miss Norma Jean," drawled the Georgia voice of

Andy, "you and I have as good as won."

And then Raggedy Ann *declared*, in a sweet voice I knew only too well, that he was right.

I wanted to throw up.

"Okay," said Soup, punching me a sharp poke in the ribs, "forget your dumb ankle, and your *heart*, and let's get ourselfs a move on."

"Where to?" I asked him.

"You'll see. Where we start from," Soup explained, "is part of our big surprise."

We unloaded Mama and Aunt Carrie and Mrs. Vinson, who went to investigate what was behind the BIG SALE sign in the window of the drygoods store. Mr. Vinson left, too, after Soup persuaded his pa that he and I would take the reins, to go find a shade spot where we'd rest the team and buckboard.

"Soup, where are we headed?"

"Just you watch."

Soup clucked the horses into a walk, around the corner where the bank was, up Elm Street, making a right turn past the grocery. He drove the buckboard along Back Street and up the long hill that overlooked the town.

He finally said, "Whoa," when we'd reached the top of Main Street Hill, the only paved street in town. It was smooth and blacktopped all the way from where we stood

to the bottom of the hill. And it looked, to me, near to
half a mile long.

"I don't like it," I said.

Soup looked at me. "Patience," he said. "Because you
are about to receive the biggest thrill of your life."

"What is it?"

"Well," said Soup, "from up here is where we start
making our grand entrance."

"And we run down the hill, as a zebra?"

"Not exactly. We don't have to run. We don't even
have to walk."

"From up here, how do we get down there?"

"Simple," said Soup. "We ride."

"In what?"

"This." Soup held up the sugar sack and smiled.

"We ride down in a *bag*?"

"Nope. Let's get dressed."

I knew it was folly to press old Soup for an answer. So I
got myself dressed. As most everything we brought was
stiff with paint, it took us longer than planned; but we
finally wiggled into our black and white burlap stripes.
Soup put the shoebox on his head. I can't say he looked
like a zebra. But he sure looked like a kid wearing a
shoebox.

Soup tied the piano wires on me for a tail and then

lowered the barrel down over my head. I didn't feel much like the back half of a zebra, and I knew I sure didn't look like one. What we looked like was probably a traveling dump. There was sawdust inside the ancient barrel, and it itched my nose. My barrel was open at both ends so that my head and arms came out the top, and my legs came out the bottom. All it had was sides and sawdust.

Soup lifted the barrel so that its top was even with the top of my head, roping it in place with twine. All I could see now was a circle of sky.

"Ready?" asked Soup.

"I'm not hiking down that long hill, Soup. My ankle can't take it."

"Don't worry. You won't have to walk an inch."

There was a long pause. "What are you doing now?" I asked, as I could hear metallic rattles.

"Opening my sack," said Soup.

Looking out through a busted stave in my barrel, I didn't believe what I saw. Soup had surely gone insane. He had pulled three things out of the sack, two of which he attached to himself.

Wow! I was too shocked to speak, even when I felt Soup strapping the third one to my bad foot.

"Sorry," said Soup, "but I could only locate three. So

you can use your good foot, to drag, in case we need a brake."

My voice sounded weak when I could finally force myself to speak, with just two words.

"Roller skates?"

TWELVE

"Soup, are you nuts?"

"That's the trouble with this world," said Soup. "Folks always confuse determination with insanity. Bend over. Good. Now hold it."

"I'm getting out of this barrel. Right now."

"You can't."

Soup was right. He had somehow quickly tied the top rim of the barrel to his back. Bent over, I couldn't seem to either straighten up or even back out of my barrel. All I could do was hang on to the back of Soup's belt, which was in front of my face. I had been roped in in more ways than one.

"I can't really see too much," my voice echoed out a yell, feeling as if I was talking only to myself. At times such as this, conversing with Luther Vinson was always a waste of breath. "All I see is a tiny hunk of the road."

"Don't worry," said Soup. "I can see."

"How? You got a shoebox on your head."

"I'm looking out through the nostrils."

"Darn you, Soup. You've got me trapped in here."

"So you wouldn't back out, Rob."

"I can't back out," I said, trying again to back out of the barrel. "You've got me tied in, haven't you? You rat."

Soup laughed. "Only to hold us together. Now to make our grand entrance. On wheels!"

"But this is crazy, Soup. I've never been on roller skates in my life."

"Don't worry. Neither have I. But I saw some kids in town doing it once and it looks real easy. Especially downhill. That makes it simpler than ice skating."

"Shouldn't we practice first? On level ground?"

"There isn't time. By now, the judges have probable seen most every costume. Except ours."

"I won't go."

Soup sighed. "Rob, do you want Norma Jean

Bissell and that Beverly Bean kid to win the prize?"

"No."

"Okay, then let's show this town a sight to remember. It isn't every day that folks get to see a zebra on roller skates. Here we go!"

If we were a sight to remember, then it was a sight that everyone would see except for me. "Can we go real slow?" I was trying to balance myself on my one sore ankle, the one that wore the roller skate. We were moving.

"We'll go slow," said Soup.

"Good."

Soup chuckled. "At first."

He was right. Even from inside the barrel I could feel that we were beginning to gather up speed. Bent forward, and peeking down through the busted slat, I saw the pavement rolling by, faster and faster. It became a black blur.

Foolishly, I tried to drag my free foot, the one without a roller skate; but it didn't slow us down. Then I knew why. Ahead of me, Luther Vinson, soon to be famed as The Mad Roller Skater of Main Street Hill, was skating forward as fast as he could. Pumping with every driving push.

"Whee!" hollered Soup. "This is fun on wheels."

Behind him, problems were rapidly compounding; I couldn't seem to master balancing on one skate and also support the barrel in my bent-over position.

"Slow down, Soup."

"I can't. We're into the steep part."

"What'll I do?"

"Wiggle your tail and try to kick like a zebra with your free foot. And, oh yes, one more thing."

"What's that?"

"Pray."

Never before had I realized that the wheels of three roller skates could roar out such a noise. And the racket grew louder with every inch we rolled. We were doomed to crash. I just felt it, all over.

"Okay," yelled Soup. "Hit the brakes."

I slammed my good foot down hard, hoping we'd somehow slow down to only one hundred miles per hour. But when my foot hit the pavement, it threw my balance off. My head jerked up and bumped the slats of my barrel, real hard.

Dust flew up my nose. I had to sneeze. So I reared back and sneezed.

"Brake!" howled Soup.

"I'm . . . *achoo* . . . trying to, Soup . . . *achoo* . . .

but I . . . *achoo* . . . can't seem to . . . *achoo*. . . . *Achoooo!"*

My last sneeze was a real bomber. It even made Soup jump.

"Rob—"

"Yeah?"

"Do you believe in God?"

"Yes!" I screamed back. I sure didn't want to cause us any *more* grief than the mess we were already in.

"Good," said Soup. "Your prayers have been heard."

"Why?" I hollered at him, between sneezes.

"Because," said Soup, "I think we just might be going to join the Methodist church. At full speed."

"Turn."

"I can't," Soup yelled back. "One of my skates is tangled with your stupid piano wire."

"No!"

Again my head smacked against the barrel. The dust was so thick that I couldn't even see what little of the road I had previously seen. I sneezed again, and again.

Soup suddenly hollered, "Look out!" But I sensed he wasn't hollering at me.

"What is it?" I wheezed.

"Hey! Get out of the way. We can't stop!"

"What are you yelling at? The Methodist church?"

"No," answered Soup. "I can't seem to make it out, but it's something else. Real big."

"Can't you *see?*"

"The doggone nostrils moved," howled Soup. "I think my head's on backward."

"Then turn it around. Somebody's got to see. I'm stuck back here in this barrel."

"Oh! . . . Oh, *no!*"

"Soup, for gosh sakes, what is it we're heading for? If it isn't the Methodist church, tell me what we're going to hit."

One of Soup's eyes must have finally lined up behind one of the zebra's nostrils because I knew, by his next scream, that Soup suddenly saw what we were about to crash into.

"What is it?" I yelled.

Soup hollered back. "It's a giant *mule.*"

"Margaret?"

"No," said Soup. "It's even bigger."

It would be difficult to claim that I was an expert on smashing into thin people like Mr. Jubert. Yet it would be my guess that anyone (or anything, even a *truck*) stops dead whenever he runs into Miss Boland.

KA-THUMP-KA-DA-BOOOOM.

I heard a very loud noise, the sound of a shattering barrel. And three people screamed: Mr. Jubert, Miss Boland, and then Soup. All I did was sneeze. Oddly enough, the only part of my body that wasn't hurting was my ankle.

Even my hair felt broken.

Opening my eyes, I saw Mr. Jubert (who was on the bottom of the pile) open his, peering around his halfmoon glasses that now dangled from one of his ears. They were swinging to and fro. Mr. Jubert appeared to be unhappy. People usually are whenever they're lying underneath Miss Boland.

Poor skinny Mr. Jubert seemed to be in a daze. Then his customary frown slowly returned. He scowled, smiled, and mumbled, "Hee haw."

The four of us were in sorry shape, but our barrel was totally in splinters. Rope and striped burlap seemed to be all over everybody. Miss Boland sat up, still dressed in the rear half of her gray mule outfit, and looked sternly down at Mr. Jubert upon whom she sat.

"Horace," she said, "I warned you to watch where we were going. I think we ran into someone."

"My main regret," snarled Mr. Jubert through clenched teeth, "is the day I ran into *you*."

Miss Boland struggled with her zipper. "Darn it, the

doggone thing is stuck," she said.

"That's *my* zipper," grunted Mr. Jubert. "And I'll thank you to leave it alone."

"Now, Horace," said Miss Boland.

"Why?" asked Mr. Jubert. "Why, for Pete's sake, is my foot in a shoebox?"

I looked at Soup who was trying to spit an object out of his mouth. It was one of our fake ears.

"What hit us?" asked Miss Boland. "It must have been a moving van."

"No," grunted Mr. Jubert. "It was a zebra. On wheels. Now will the three of you please get off, so that I'll know that whatever is left is me."

"I can't move," groaned Soup.

"It's the piano wire," I said. "We're all snarled up, like a backlash on a fishing reel." I was lying on one of Soup's roller skates and it didn't feel too soft.

Miss Boland was the first to roll off Mr. Jubert, and it sure must have been a welcomed relief for *him*.

"Let's hurry," she said. "Horace, I can't wait to see if we won a prize."

Mr. Jubert moaned. "The only prize I deserve," he snorted, "is the one they ought to hand out for being the biggest jackass."

"Cheer up," Miss Boland told him. "At least we're still alive enough to participate in the rest of the festivities."

"Yeah," said Mr. Jubert, "if they hold 'em at the hospital."

"Well," said Miss Boland, "it certainly is a lucky thing that I'm a nurse."

Mr. Jubert snorted. "It sure is, considering all the tomfool *damage* you cause."

The three of us got up and then helped poor Mr. Jubert to his feet. He wobbled a bit at first, stepped on one of Soup's rollerskates, and fell flat. Miss Boland couldn't help laughing. It made me happy to see the grownups having so much fun.

The judges awarded the prizes, in reverse order.

Soup and I had to admit that we were pleased to see Miss Boland and Mr. Jubert limp forward and take third.

I was less pleased, however, when second place was awarded to Beverly Bean and Norma Jean Bissell. But that was only the beginning. The one event that really got me sore on the day of the Mardy Grah was when the big silver trophy was given, as first prize for the best costume.

"Rob, it had to happen," said Soup, as the two of us watched the winner accept first prize.

You can't beat Janice as a gorilla.

photo by Dorrie

Robert Newton Peck and his pet skunk, Shalimar

ROBERT NEWTON PECK has written twenty-nine books for both young readers and adults since his highly praised first novel, A DAY NO PIGS WOULD DIE was published in 1973. SOUP ON WHEELS is his fifth book about those mischief-packing pals Soup and Rob—"Vermont's answers to Huck and Tom" says *Language Arts.* "I only write about what I know . . ." says Peck. "My SOUP books reflect my boyhood on a Vermont farm."

Robert Newton Peck lives with his wife, who is a librarian and painter, and their two children in Longwood, Florida, where he is the director of Rollins College Writers Conference.

103